Una Woods lives in Belfast, Ireland where she was born and raised.

Her first published poems and short stories appeared In the late 1970's in the New Writing Page of The Irish Press, edited by David Marcus.

The Dark Hole Days, a novella and short stories was published by *Blackstaff Press* in 1984.

Over the years she has contributed stories and poems to various anthologies in Ireland, The UK and USA.

Other *Una Woods* books published by *Ashtrees* are:

Afternoons, selected poems, 2006.

An Icicle for an eye, notepoems, 2011.

2 Plays, Grace before meals; For want of the call, 2013.

Splintered vision, selected poems, 2016.

An earlier version of Chapter 1 of **Mr and Mrs McKeown** appeared as a short story in the Phoenix Book of Short Stories, edited by David Marcus, 1997.

Mr and Mrs McKeown

the accidental maze

by Una Woods

First published   2010
Re-issued 2019 Ashtrees
Ashtreespress@gmail.com

ISBN 978-0-9575858-9-8

Chapters

The letter

There was no-one in the parlour. The light fluttered like a heart, then it whimpered like a sound. The wallpaper peeled in places. The church-bell rang.

Mr McKeown grabbed his hat from the hall-stand. Mercy be to God, he said.

Mrs McKeown moved about in the kitchen. Out through the window the yard fell instant. Like an atomic silence. Inside Mrs McKeown moved an ornament slightly into place. The front door closed. At the centre of the bang Mrs McKeown paused. She looked around the walls.

Mr McKeown peered into the monastery glow, his hands behind his back, stooped forward. Celebration stopped short as incense. There were no seats. Standing at the back Mr McKeown joined in with the prayers, rolled his eyes to the high ceiling, supplicating.

Outside in the street the deadened drone could be heard. A bicycle rang but it made no difference, slates were more like it weakened as they were by evening light. There were no birds. So much was happening the evening shortened, drained through stained-glass. Light on its last legs.

Mrs McKeown moved her parlour curtain. In the flattening gap children glided. Mrs McKeown fixed her eyes on the hidden scene. From where she was the shimmer-stopped evening played like awakening.   Frail voices sudden as brick, then ripples.

Mr McKeown got up after the blessing and brushed the knees of his trousers. The organist launched into music that caused chaos on the altar.   As people made their way out into the straight light their clothes were already drab. Mr McKeown amongst them stopped and looked around, as if at an alien race. That surprise on his face.   Merciful Jesus, he said rocking on his heels. Tut, tut. Then he vanished out through the gates and into the dim-sparked evening streets. All the rest went their separate ways.

The door closed.   Merciful heavens, Mr McKeown said placing his hat on the hook. They were the only two sounds in the house. When he broke into the kitchen like a man home his wife slipped out of the shadows. Then when he went to open a cupboard door she whispered, Don't touch that. He looked up at her, still crouched. Till you've washed your hands, she whispered.
Jesus, Mary and Joseph, Mr McKeown said wringing his hands.
Later he sat in his chair counting coins. Children could be heard faint in the street.
Mrs McKeown came from the scullery. Give me a penny, she said to her husband.
I'm not sure I can afford it now, Mr McKeown said looking down at the coins. I was going to give it to the monastery.

Mrs McKeown said nothing. She went over to the sideboard and lifted a tin. She took the lid off and poked in it then replaced the tin and hurried out to the door. She barely opened it but drew the attention of a child by wagging one finger.

I'll give you a penny if you go away, she said.

The child took the penny and went back to her friends. They moved a few doors down the street. Lamp-light flickered just on where the street hung before darkness.

The next day pale quiet opened on houses. Bleary morning basked on slate. Weak-lit clouds hovered thin as another day. Mrs McKeown walked into the parlour. Light tinkled on the net curtain where her fretful eyes fixed. No-one sees me from here, she thought.   Then things happened together, as if they were life. Mrs McKeown began to move like a participant. First I must go out to the shop, she thought, and get some eggs for the breakfast. It's a lovely morning, clouds make the sun possible.

Immaculate Mother of God, Mr McKeown ejaculated coming down the stairs. Saint Anthony and all the saints.

Mrs McKeown waited till he had gone into the kitchen then she slipped out into the hall, took her coat from the hall-stand, tiptoed down the hall and out through the front door. When she looked down the street she saw futures flickering in wait. She chose the one that lay ahead. I must walk here, she thought. Beyond the corner stopped but only out of sight. Mrs McKeown took each step against the air that lightened her passage. Dizzy bits of dust glistened against the road's dull edge. Half a dozen eggs, she whispered over to herself, and a couple of soda farls. She reached the corner and continued on.

Where's that blessed woman, Mr McKeown said out loud. He walked in his stooped way into the scullery, leaning forward as if in the dim glimmer he might see her. Then he rocked on his heels, hands behind his back. He shook his head. Lord the night, he murmured, give me patience.
He turned back into the kitchen and went over to a picture of the Sacred Heart hanging on the wall. He lit a small red lamp underneath it, and kneeling down before it began to pray fervently.

Mrs McKeown stopped in the doorway. Preserve us, she whispered rolling her eyes. She went into the scullery with the groceries. Mr McKeown finished his prayers, got up and brushed the knees of his trousers. He went into the scullery and opened the door out to the yard. What's it like out, eh? he asked his wife.
A bit dull, Mrs McKeown said putting an egg into a small saucepan of cold water, then added turning up the gas, but there's a break in the clouds.

Later that morning Mr McKeown was out doing his laundry round.

Mrs McKeown took a chair out into the yard and sat in the early sun. This is the ticket, she thought, so long as nobody comes to the back door. She took a letter from her apron pocket and opening it out began to read it. Her most pressing thoughts when she came to the end of the page were, How did she come to think of me? How did she get my address? And then, How can I reply? Like the silent aftermath, the lone survivor of an explosion she read again the words of warmth from an old friend. She felt herself beginning to shake. Then she shuffled herself up in her chair until her body was erect. She stared at the back door a minute then quickly folded the letter back into the envelope and stuffed it into her pocket.

It's too late, she thought defiantly, I'm almost pleased to show her.

Mrs McKeown got up from her chair, lifted it and carried it back into the kitchen. Then, in the spirit of resentment she plotted to clean the house from top to bottom.

I'll show her, she thought on her hands and knees scrubbing the scullery tiles, I'll show her what's become of me. Who does she think she is anyway?

Outside, the dull air flickered then dissolved. All that could be heard in the distance were the numb sounds of every day. Inside, the soapy scrub angered hope. It was all she could do to continue, against knowledge, moving the bucket like a pained clang across the floor. Now and again the letter made little crumpled noises in her pocket.

Unless I could go, Mrs McKeown thought suddenly. She knelt upright on the dry tiles. Unless I could go and see her, sure I've lived like a fool.

Mrs McKeown's throat fluttered like the last piece of snow on a sunny yard wall. Or the first primrose in a lonely country lane.

Mr McKeown said goodbye to the nuns at the nursing-home door. Then he drove his van down the long driveway, through trees with shades of brown and yellow like nothing on earth. Nothing on the treeless street where he lived, the lamps ordinary, lit or unlit. He drove through the strange golden glimmer and out onto the stuttering road. When able he turned left. Of all that's good and wonderful, he muttered to himself. Saint Brigid and Saint Patrick. People walked in both directions and the light spread and flattened on the pavements.

Ha-ha, Mr McKeown laughed and shook his head. Who would have believed it? Who in their right minds, that I would be with the laundry all this time.

The spire of the church rose ahead, it narrowed up to a weak sky as if to tip liquid identity.

Mr McKeown's eyes stared at the road beyond, height swam in their reflection of light. When he turned into the streets he felt eternity as solid as the houses on either side, his life vindicated, his years in the laundry.

Mercy be to the heavens, he said. Praise be to God.

Children played at doorways, their shouts rang short.

Mrs McKeown felt a different person. It was easy. Silence was enough, and walls as thin as years. When she walked on the floor the ice of imagination smoothed her way. She touched things as if she controlled them. The suddenness of freedom came back to her, it was the same place, after all this time. She took the letter from her pocket and out of its envelope. She smoothed the paper on her knee then read the words like magic. The address at the top of the page was shocking and exciting. Saudi Arabia. I could get the plane, she thought. I could fly out, sure these streets are dead.

She slipped into the parlour and looked through the net curtains at the soundless grey, no hope of reawakening, why would she stay? Then a reminder as dull as prevention the drone of the laundry-van. It pulled up outside the door. In the stone-smooth grey of afternoon Mr McKeown jumped down onto the pavement. The sound of his feet closed the scene, the future here impossible.

Mrs McKeown heard the thud of confirmation then fixed the corner of the curtain slightly. Brick flickered on the far side of the street.

Divine light, Mr McKeown said as he came to the door. When he was in the hall and had closed the door behind him he said, Merciful Jesus and his Holy Mother. Then his feet walked sure as yesterday on oilcloth.

Mrs McKeown stood still by the window, rigid with detachment, imminent collapse balanced around her. Then from the scullery came the sound of water bouncing on stone.

Good, Mrs McKeown sighed, he's washing his hands.

When she appeared in the kitchen door he said without looking up, Ah, now, sure the nuns were in good form today, what? He wrung his hands under the gushing water. Two bags of laundry. Tut, tut.

Two bags, imagine that. Mrs McKeown shook her head then added, It's a lot for nuns right enough. When she saw Mr McKeown staring at the back door she said, Use the kitchen paper, I've washed the towel. The words fell on the clean floor where she looked down out of habit. Then as if nothing had changed Mr McKeown crumpled up the wet kitchen paper and threw it into the bin.

They passed each other on the scullery step almost touching.

Saudi Arabia, Mrs McKeown thought.

Lord the night, Mr McKeown said.

Days merged into winter. Cold air gripped the fading light like a brick wall. Mrs McKeown got no further. Day after day secret thoughts swam in circles until they met the dusk and disappeared. She could not make plans.

One day she put pen to paper. Seated at the kitchen table a fiasco of feeble light on roofs beyond. She stared ahead at the back wall, something further, further than wall. What she had to say was a hung memory, it took up the whole evening. When she looked down at the page she couldn't think what to write. Then words came stilted as daily chores. As the odd light in a window coming on, the blind abruptly closed. What could she reveal? 'I' seemed too much after all the years of hiding from it. 'I' closed before her on the page. It could not live up to the expectations of the new writing-pad and envelopes. And Mr McKeown due home from the laundry in no time. Like a rabbit darting its head out of a burrow only to hear the sound that threatened its whole life Mrs McKeown snapped the writing-pad closed and scuttled over to put it at the back of the drawer.

The house stunned into evening. Mrs McKeown's eyes stared out the kitchen window at nothing moving. But the moment moved imperceptibly so that the faint fidget of dusk seemed everywhere. In comparison to the evening light

wasted on slate. To the fixed glaze of the high
yard wall. When she touched the letter through
the wool of her cardigan pocket the crumpled
petals opened in the sun. The house sank slowly
in the growing glimmer but when she tried to put
it into action she couldn't move. Then from a
street behind a voice deadly as unbroken days.
Mrs McKeown hurried to put on the kitchen
light.

Tomorrow, she thought, I'll go to the Travel
Agents.

Sweet Virgin Mary, Mr McKeown said as he
hung his brown laundry-coat on the back of the
kitchen door. He took some coins out of one of
the pockets and counted them. The infant Jesus,
he said shaking his head.

Mrs McKeown set a heavy pan down on the
stove like the end of marriage. Then she came as
far as the scullery doorway.

Is there an atlas in the house? she said more
inaudibly than she meant.

Mr McKeown was banging coins in his pocket.
He swung round.

Speak up, woman, he said, speak up! Then he
looked at his watch. He flung his arms in the air.
Jesus, Mary and Joseph, he exclaimed, I'm doing
the collection.

I said, Mrs McKeown raised her voice just above
the sound of bacon frying, Is there an atlas in the
house?

Mr McKeown rocked on his heels. Ha-ha, an atlas, he laughed. When did I last see an atlas. Then he frowned across at her. Why, are you thinking of sending some money off to the missions? Do you want to know where Africa is? He rushed out of the room and up the stairs. Christ on the cross, he could be heard saying, Mary Magdalene at his feet. Soon he moved about the room above as if the heavens rumbled, the house below waited in anticipation. Mrs McKeown turned the bacon with the small knife. Bits of fat spat like secrets exploding where she stood on the spot.

The front door banged. Mr McKeown looked up and down the dark street, lamp-lit with reverberation, a still yellow glow. Lord have mercy, he said, beating his chest. Then he lurched across the road and into the entry opposite by way of a short-cut. Christ have mercy, he said in the entry. There was no light save where the street dimmed ahead. Mr McKeown hurried out to the dim opening. Opposite, two young girls were tying a thick rope onto a lamp-post, the stark side of amazement, their voices hushed, their faces raised in the ghost-glow. Suffer the little children, Mr McKeown said as he passed by.
Hallo Mr McKeown, they answered in unison, they sang.
Houses all around joined in in silence. In solid dark. In the scale of things they stood on either

side. Shadows made no difference. Then out onto the main road suddenly where Mr McKeown glanced up and down as if mankind could be lying in wait, its intention withheld door to door. Tall lights were more like it leaving dark as it was. Pray for us sinners, Mr McKeown said as he turned abruptly left. A few people walked ahead. Now and at the hour of our death, Mr McKeown said in a low voice. He blessed himself.

Mrs McKeown walked past the Travel Agents for the second time.   Through the large window genuine travellers were chatting to clerks. Coloured posters showed the blues and yellows of sea and sand and cloudless skies. People on the pavement ignored Mrs McKeown, or looked at her with hardened faces. I'm out of place here, she thought, where people don't know me. They pass like strangers, far from where I live. She stopped and looked into a shoe-shop then moved slightly to right and left pretending to examine different pairs of shoes. But how can I get to Saudi Arabia without going into the Travel Agents? she thought. Without asking questions that will give me away?   Without hearing answers that make everything impossible?

Mrs McKeown hurried past the Travel Agents without as much as glancing in. She reached the corner where opposite, the City Hall rose bare in the morning sun. It closed its door on the bright sky, even to pass it seemed impossible. I'm so small in the city, Mrs McKeown thought, and the bus for home is almost out of reach. There it is at the side of the City Hall. When able she crossed the wide road diagonally, almost beaten by the desert cement. Her feet sank one after the other in it, her progress a pilgrimage to a queue.

Once on the bus, light flooded the sky just where buildings parted. I'm on my way, Mrs McKeown sighed. She smiled then poked in her purse for the right fare.

Santa Claus

Sweet Mother of God, Mr McKeown said throwing his head back like an idea. It's nearly Christmas. He stood in the middle of the kitchen lit-up at three o'clock in the afternoon. The saints above, he added and sighed. He shook his trouser pockets.

Mrs McKeown followed a shovel up the yard. Cold air hit a brick wall then flattened vertical. Mrs McKeown continued heedless, as if the shovel was empty. The light above rooftops departed day after day, slates glowed only gradually. Mrs McKeown lowered her eyes. She closed the back door and came in from the scullery.
Three pieces of coal, Mr McKeown remarked barely glancing at the shovel. Woman dear, he added.
Mrs McKeown threw the coal onto the fire. She hit the shovel on the side of the chimney. There was little or no heat in the kitchen.
The infant Jesus, Mr McKeown ejaculated shaking his head. Christmas is upon us.
'Deed'n' aye, Mrs McKeown murmured. She passed by with the shovel. She sat it at the scullery door as if the less sound the better then adjusted it slightly. At the end of the scrape she stood up straight, looked around the barren shelves. Cold shivered under the back door

sneaking winter in. Mrs McKeown tightened the string of her apron.

Mr McKeown laughed at the bare bulb. Ha-ha. He smacked his knee. In under God, he said, Santa Claus. He rocked on his heels. Mrs McKeown turned in the scullery door, the air turned to feather, pale green a poor substitute. She rolled her eyes up, then sighed. She came across the scullery step. Mr McKeown peered at her through his eyebrows.

What does he want me to say? Mrs McKeown thought, the patterned wallpaper no escape though directly opposite.

Did you hear me? Mr McKeown said as she passed him by. Santa Claus. He bent down in mid-air.

The very thing, Mrs McKeown said low making no progress. Something fundamental stood between.

God and his holy mother, Mr McKeown said swivelling on his heels as though something sudden had happened. His wife was nearing the door. He put his hand into his inside pocket and withdrew some notes. The sound stopped Mrs McKeown in her tracks. She stood staring at the closed door and heard the sound of flicking behind like an ancient rite her head held high.

When she turned abruptly the notes were gone.

The Lord is my shepherd, Mr McKeown said. He had his hands joined. The lamp below the picture of the Sacred Heart glowed like a drop of pure blood, not long on.

Mrs McKeown balanced on the parlour floor. The unlived-in air dazzled, furniture faded defiantly, age no barrier. Outside, a hint of sunlight delayed on roofs, dusk waited unhurried as the next moment. It's a lovely evening, Mrs McKeown thought, the net curtain barely blurs the window. She leant forward and tugged the corner of the curtain. When she let it go a vacant earthquake bounced back up. Mrs McKeown steadied on her feet and heard the frail sound of children on their way from school.

Mr McKeown stood back and looked at the chair. He shook his head. In the name of all that's good and wonderful, he said, I mind the time when chairs were chairs. He bent down and tugged at the soft seat, with difficulty he prised it from the base. Agitated he let it spring back down. Listening for sounds he fumbled in his inside pocket, with his right hand he removed a bunch of notes, with his left, as though in harmony he lifted the seat of the chair again. He stuffed the notes underneath as far as he could then pretended he was doing nothing.
Sweet heavens above, he said brushing the lapel of his jacket with the backs of his fingers. Ha-ha, he laughed. Santa Claus.
Mrs McKeown stood in the hall and glanced two ways. Then she turned left and went towards the

kitchen.   Behind her, outside voices thickened and went strange.   Mrs McKeown was alerted to something immediate or always, pausing made no difference, there was nothing to decide.   She turned the handle of the kitchen door.   It was the only sound in the house.   Unless I could make a noise, Mrs McKeown thought, sure I've been quiet too long.

The kitchen light displayed the space between, what she saw wasn't there, it took up the whole room. Mr McKeown at the other side got up from his knees.   He dusted the legs of his trousers. Saint Nicholas, he said.   Mercy me.

Mrs McKeown crossed over to the scullery.   She hummed as she went.   Something indiscernible, something old or made- up.   The sound had the ring of reluctance before it stopped.   She turned in the scullery door.

Do you remember that old song-book? she asked raising her voice more than she meant.

Mr McKeown had his head cocked to the side. Now he took a step back as if hit.   He planted one foot after the other on the oilcloth.   Old song-book? he said loudly. Old song-book? You mean hymn-book, don't you? You're one of those that mumble the words, eh?   Ha-ha.   He threw his hands in the air then brought them down and smacked both knees.   He looked at his watch. The angel Gabriel, he said.   Tut-tut.   Mrs McKeown opened a cupboard and stared inside further than the sparse shelves. She held the door still, then into her vision came two red tomatoes, a piece of cheese, a half-dozen eggs and a small loaf of white bread. The house came alive. Mrs McKeown chose life.   She reached into the cupboard and began taking things out for the tea. When the cupboard door banged, action deadened while she busied herself away. At the sink she turned a tomato round and round in her hand while the water splashed on it. Good, she thought, it should be clean now. When she raised her eyes and looked through the small window light crumbled in smooth swathes, the corner in plain shadow. Mrs McKeown had nothing but the constant change to go by.

Mr McKeown jingled his pockets. He shook his head. Then he began to rush about. Jesus, Mary and Joseph, he exaggerated.   The novena.   He hurried out into the hall, grabbed his coat from the hall-stand, swung it over his arm, then his hat which he placed on his head. As he hurried to the door he said, Miraculous Mother of God.

When the front door banged Mrs McKeown stood in the middle of the aftermath on the kitchen floor. She had a dishcloth in her hand but it was no solution. She wiped the wooden table then a gem of a thought twinkled in her head. The old songs again, she thought, followed by, but who would I sing to? How would I get it going?

Suddenly the house hushed like an audience, through the window the darkening sky, the stars, if they shone, extenuating circumstances.   Mrs

McKeown waited to begin, motionless with control. She almost smiled, her eyes unseeing with attention. She sang in a girlish voice:

When like the dawning day
Eileen Aroon
Love sends his early ray
Eileen Aroon
What makes his dawning glow
Changeless through joy and woe
Only the constant know
Eileen Aroon

Were she no longer true
Eileen Aroon
What would her lover do
Eileen Aroon
Fly with a broken chain
Far o'er the bounding main
Never to love again
Eileen Aroon
Youth must in time decay
Eileen Aroon
Beauty must fade away
Eileen Aroon
Castles are sacked in war
Chieftains are scattered far
Truth is a fixed star
Eileen Aroon

Only when she tailed off on the last line did her cheeks burn with embarrassment. She could not

believe the acoustics in her own house.   She
looked around the walls which were deafening,
then going about as normal seemed peculiar.
From a street behind, a sound resounded like
news from abroad but Mrs McKeown had only a
remote interest in foreign affairs. She opened the
back door and threw tea-leaves into the drain in
one go. Good, she thought, I don't have to rinse
the teapot again.   Anyway I'm obsessed with
singing.   Involuntarily she sang the first line of
another song then stopped.   She stood still, the
teapot in both hands, listened across walls, then
slipped back into the house.

Mr McKeown stopped before he turned onto the
main road.   He stooped, hands behind back and
peered down the road.   Pools of pavement
shimmered on the spot, terraced houses were
breathtaking down to the corner.   Mr McKeown
could not believe his eyes. Praise be to God, he
said. And his holy Mother. Then he swerved left
in the direction of the monastery.
Ahead of him darkness swayed in and out of light
or it was the other way round.   Anyway it
dissolved up to the mountain into pure night. Mr
McKeown knew the way. He shook his head. I
declare to God, he whispered, the monastery.
Saved on his feet he lurched forward taking the
middle of the pavement.   Then a bit in front he
saw a figure coming out of a side-street, a figure
risen out of shadow though it stayed the same.
The night air clamped the shock.   Mr McKeown

quickened his step.   The bakery on his left loomed closed, on his right the long factory wall. In between, Mr McKeown's spirit soared with no escape. He rejoiced several times on the way.

He stopped suddenly. Oh, Jesus Christ, he struck himself on the chest. Then he opened the buttons of his long coat and put his hand into his jacket pocket. He withdrew a gold watch. He moved into the lamplight and examining the watch he ran his thumb over the back of it. I must get that melted down, he thought, and give it to the monastery. He replaced the watch in his pocket, patted it, closed his coat and hurried on. Just at the point of crossing the road to head up the street that led to the monastery he caught up with the figure. The man raised his head by way of greeting. Man dear, Mr McKeown said with a mock gasp, you gave me a fright. Then he added, I knew it was you. The man chuckled. Santa Claus, he said.

Mrs McKeown's head was away. So much was in it she didn't know where to turn. She turned towards the kitchen door. When she put her hand on the handle she felt paralysed so momentous was her thought.   Her chest swelled into her throat, she felt the strain in her eyes. Everything could happen any minute, already it was out of control. Songs, gatherings, filled nights. She turned abruptly and looked around the wasted kitchen, slightly hazy. She sighed and turned back to the door. But where do you start? she thought. What's the first move?

Mrs McKeown walked out into the hall, turned right and stepped towards the front door. When she opened it the cold air broke in.   Mrs McKeown took a deep breath.

Then the street moved into distance the houses opposite only a few feet away. The monastery bell rang. Mrs McKeown stood where she was, there was no hurry. The silence of a stopped bell rang on rooftops, no-one was about. When she looked down the street, lamps were steadfast in their change, their light just holding onto the pavement. She adjusted her position and looked again.   Cold gleamed on brick, doors were closed. Her eyes moved around the empty street. Are these the people who would come to listen? she thought. No, other people, other people far away. The idea dangled mere hope, it caught the winter air permanently. Mrs McKeown huddled one more time against the door frame. She considered everything then turned in a hurry and went in. As soon as she closed the door a song burst out, though low enough:

After the ball is over
After the break of morn
After the dancers' leaving
After the stars are gone
Many a heart is aching
If you could read them all
 Many the hopes that have shattered

After the ball-.

Mr McKeown clasped his hands in front of him. He swayed back and forth. His eyes glinted. He was standing on the monastery steps looking down towards the gates, the streets below stayed put.   Lamb of God, Mr McKeown said in amazement.   Who takest away the sins of the world. He was on the top step in no hurry to go down. People passed by on either side. They stepped, heads down into the hard night, cold air flew away to the sky where it stopped as stars. Mr McKeown had a minute to spare, he bowed his head. Hark the herald angels sing, he said. Well I never. Ha-ha. He stood on as though alone in the midst of people who gave him comfort. He raised his head with pride. The crowds grew thinner all around. Still the organ played out carols although quietness crept up from the city streets. Suddenly Mr McKeown wondered, he shook his head.   Almighty and everlasting God, he said. He put his hands in his pockets and felt around.   Two coins clinked softly in one pocket. Tut, tut. He went down the steps. A few feet on he remembered something and   paused.   His   eyes   narrowed   with concentration, the organ a back-drop.   Then his coat swung as he hurried on out through the gates and down the gradual decline of streets like an accidental maze, every end open.   When he thumped past windows the odd Christmas tree sparkled, a false dead-end. Mr McKeown hurried on though mostly looking at the ground. Occasionally he shook his head. Once he threw his arms in the air.   Mother of God, he commented then reached the main road.

Mrs McKeown looked into the box. She was out of breath from hurrying up and down the stairs. Once the decorations are up, she thought still looking into the box in solitude.   It was the moment before she put them up, before everything was transformed. She raised her head and turning it slowly considered the three walls. There was no alternative, she looked forward to the diversion, not facing life on her own. Then she straightened herself and went over to the sideboard to look for small nails from last year. Before she opened the drawer she stopped still and thought of Christmas.   Then when she poked in the drawer the nails weren't there.   Neither were they in the other drawer.   A song was opportune. She stood with the drawers open and sang in a light, delayed voice:

Sleigh bells ring, are you listening
In the lane, snow is glistening
A beautiful sight
We're happy tonight
Walking in a winter wonderland

Gone away is the bluebird
Here to stay is a new bird

He sings a love song
As we go along
Walking in a winter wonderland

In the meadow we can build a snowman
Then pretend that he's parson Brown
He'll say are you married, we'll say no man
But you can do the job if you're on time-

Mrs McKeown stopped abruptly, the presence of silence in the house a shock. She bowed her head and waited for the future, when it came she looked up at the clock. The novena's over and all, she thought, and I'm nowhere. She shut the drawers and went into a little cubby-hole under the stairs with no light. She felt around in the dark where things used to be but when she touched something she knew it was useless.
Unless, she thought, they're in the box. She paused in the dark then emerged blinded in time to hear the front door close.

Mr McKeown walked up the hall. He whistled a tune that had the air of return then stopped by the hook, took his hat and coat off and hung them up. The saints above, he said. He adjusted his jacket on his shoulders then paused and cocked his head at what sounded like scraping across the kitchen floor. Just before he opened the door he murmured, Santa Claus. Then in the blaring light his body swayed back though his feet stood still.

God take care of us woman, he said. Mrs McKeown was sitting on the chair as if she had done nothing wrong, the walls bare as denial. What's that noise under me, she whispered, like paper.

Och now sure the carols were a joy, Mr McKeown said. Tut, tut, you should have been there. He glanced under the chair then made no sound sighing. Mrs McKeown sat on a minute, her body superfluous, moving in itself admission. I'm sorry I missed it, she said, then murmured, the least blameworthy though not meaning to follow it up, I was looking for small nails.

Ha-ha, Mr McKeown laughed moving into the middle of the floor. That's a thing and a half. Small nails indeed.

Mrs McKeown sat stubbornly, not singing a note on purpose. Mr McKeown confronted, For the love of God, looking at the fire. He rushed into the scullery, grabbed the shovel and scurried out into the yard. Mrs McKeown stood up and moved to the window. Pulling the blind up slightly she watched him pointlessly. Coal crashed in the dark as if to end it all, then there were footsteps. But she had already moved away from the blind into the consistency of camouflage.

Later that evening Mr and Mrs McKeown sat in the kitchen before a low fire. They both felt slight heat on their shins. Mrs McKeown scoured the evening newspaper. Every time she turned a page Mr McKeown startled, What? and shook his head. He held onto each arm of the chair ready to get up suddenly. Mrs McKeown had no idea when. When she was perusing the Sports page at the back he jumped up. Jesus, Mary and Joseph, he agitated. The crib. Mrs McKeown stared at the paper for dear life as her husband rushed from the kitchen and up the stairs. I could join the choral society, she thought. Then she sat erect in her chair, the newspaper a pastime on her knee. The rummaging in an upstairs room removed her from the scene.

Mr McKeown stood in the doorway with the box outstretched. Mrs McKeown knew what he meant, the few feet between only a moment's suspense, the night outside about to join in, space included. Mrs McKeown controlled her movements. She rose, set the paper on the table nearby and crossing the floor took the box from her husband. On the hall table, she said as if it was nothing. As she passed him by in the doorway Mr McKeown commented, Star of Bethlehem. He brushed dust off his hands.
When Mrs McKeown was setting the figures down carefully, building the story, Mr McKeown stood behind. Remember, not the kings yet, he advised. Ha-ha. He rocked on his heels. Mrs McKeown set the three kings down in line. But the kings didn't come until after- Mr McKeown anguished. Every year they get lost, Mrs McKeown interrupted, then added adjusting the

infant in the manger for the benefit of the visitors, remember to wash the dust off your hands.

Very close to Christmas Mr McKeown had a parcel under his arm. He walked towards his house in secret. The Lord only knows, he speculated. He shook his head. When he stopped at his front door to fumble for his key the parcel grew difficult under one arm. He set it on the windowsill, stood back in the night and exclaimed, Oh, Jesus. Then he bundled it into the house.

In the kitchen Mrs McKeown imagined things. The decorations made a difference otherwise the new year would come and the walls would be the same. When she saw the brown parcel she resented it already. What does it think it is, she thought, even before it was opened. Mr McKeown teased out a laugh. Ho-ho ho, he said. Then he pulled the paper apart and they both looked down at red cloth separately. Mr McKeown said, Guess, whereupon Mrs McKeown gave him one look and turned her back. She walked into the scullery and moved a cup along the shelf.

Mr McKeown came to the scullery step. In the name of God, he said. He bent down pleading into the glimmer. Then Mrs McKeown put on an act, the scullery the perfect setting.

What's wrong with Santa Claus for dear's sake, Mr McKeown begged.

I don't know what I would do without my singing, Mrs McKeown thought.

Mr McKeown remained stooped for some time awaiting an answer, his wife considered which side of him to squeeze past to start afresh. The single decoration on the far wall beckoned but she was going further.

I've to go a message before it's too late, she said finally. She untied the string of her apron, pulled it over her head and hung it on a hook on the back door. She eased herself past on the scullery step. Mr McKeown straightened himself as far as he could. Christ the night, he said.

Mrs McKeown slipped over to the chair and prised the cushion up. She withdrew one note. Mr McKeown swung round in the doorway. He shook his head. Tut, tut, he bemoaned then added, Good King Wenceslas.

Do you know where I could get a stamp? Mrs McKeown asked.

A stamp! Mr McKeown exclaimed. A stamp! He stared at the note in her hand.

Mrs McKeown hurried on out into the hall and took her coat from the hook.

I told them, Mr McKeown said after her, you could sew it up on the machine. He looked across at the red cloth on the table.

Mrs McKeown's feet sounded on the hall oilcloth. Then the front door closed.

Sure she'll never get a stamp at this hour of the night, what? Mr McKeown reassured himself. He stood looking around the kitchen a moment then hurried over to the picture of the Sacred Heart with a piece of holly on the top. He raised the bottom of it out from the wall and examined behind it then went to the armchair and prising up the seat withdrew the remainder of the notes. He carried them over to the picture of the Sacred Heart and placed them carefully between it and the wall. He secured the picture in place then stepped back and regarded it nervously. When he felt confident enough he blessed himself and knelt down. Oh Holy Father, have mercy on her, he prayed rolling his eyes to the heavens.

After considering a moment on the doorstep Mrs McKeown turned right. Dark widened its winter between houses, rooftops lay bare with affirmation. Mrs McKeown took it to heart, her coat unbuttoned like a carefree person. She walked on the earth as if it was flat, straight ahead void, she had scarcely the weight to hold her down. Windows glinted with shock in the side of her eye, her face already numb with cold. Then she came to the parochial hall where light splashed out on the pavement. Singing like strangers came from deep within. Mrs McKeown paused before going into the light, considered the effect of being seen. Once I step in, she thought, the instrument-tuned voices streets ahead. She stepped off the dark edge and landed in the

doorway on the same level. On the left a booth
had been set up, Santa's Grotto written above.
She passed it by and wandered around in the
dank hallway, the cold tiles no better. Ahead of
her an inner door was shut. Behind it and maybe
behind another door the voices climbed and
swooped, enclosed as one other.

There was no-one around to ask. Mrs McKeown
turned relieved for today. Anyway it's too near
Christmas, she thought stepping out towards the
cold night. Sure it's already all rehearsed, I'll
join fresh in the new year. She pulled her coat
around her. She stood in the doorway a moment.
On the far side of the street a man walked by like
the shadow of a friend.
Mrs McKeown compared it to everyone she had
ever known then left the doorway and headed on
down to the corner shop to get change for the
stamp machine.

Heading back up her street she checked the
journey of the little book of stamps in her pocket.
It was air mail. On either side of the street,
houses blocked out the dark. In her head she
practised her best song before she reached her
door.

The sponsored walk

The afternoon slunk in through the window but it
found no hiding place on the kitchen floor.
Outside, the yard wall choked in sun that faded
years ago to brick. In the corner a cobweb had
nothing to do, it glistened dust and trembled in
the still. Mrs McKeown had her two arms the
one length, it was the time of day between.
When she moved she balanced on light, memory
thin on the ground. Then renewing herself she
walked proudly to the scullery door. I take every
opportunity, she thought, how else would I keep
going? Ahead of her, sunlight wounded surfaces,
glass shimmered after everything else. Mrs
McKeown stopped to consider her position. At
the same time distant sounds dreaded city life,
then lived it. Two steps and she was at the sink.
She turned on the tap. I'll rinse out a few things,
she thought, then I'll have the afternoon free.
When she scrunched a tea-towel in and out of the
soapy water her thoughts wandered. Then she
rinsed it until the water was clear, wrung it in her
hands, twisted it so tight that not one drop of
water oozed. Out at the line she stood, her hands
graceful as dancers on the wire where the tea-
towel hung. The still yard air smacked of
solution. Suddenly children's voices held life-to-
the-full at bay. I never made a sound, Mrs
McKeown thought as they passed the door.
Mrs McKeown blushed as she sneaked back into
the house as if seeing herself in the mirror. I'm

ridiculous in the eyes of a child, she thought.
Then before depression set in she had an idea.
Maybe I could prove myself, she thought, sure
I've been ashamed too long.

Mr McKeown stood outside the Boys' Training
Home and put his head back.   Almighty and
merciful God, he said.   He breathed in air that
came all the way down the Black mountain, he
was nearly at the top, the sun tinkered with
houses in a valley below.   Mr McKeown stood in
his brown laundry coat and marvelled.   Well,
well, well, he said, shaking his head.   He had his
hands in his pockets but that was no restriction.
As if to prove it he turned slowly full-circle.   The
limits of distance blurred in a trance, it might
have been Castlereagh.   Ha-ha, he said in a tone
more suited to the other side of the street.
Miraculous!   Then he looked up to where a silent
procession of white clouds moved across the sky.
He started at the sound of clumping feet.   He put
his hand on his heart.   Deliver us, he said.   A line
of boys in twos walked out from the side of the
home.   Two brothers accompanied them.   From
evil, Mr McKeown added.   He took a step back
though he was not in the way.   When they
marched past his laundry van he held his breath
not to break the rhythm, then when their feet
dimmed down the long path he moved back out
to his former spot.   Hosanna in the highest!   he
declared .   He shook his head.   The path below
was empty.   Then a door opened behind him.   Mr

McKeown swung round. A brother stood in the doorway holding a large bag. Mr McKeown put his hands behind his back and stooped forward. He peered a moment then threw up his arms in astonishment.   Ah, Brother Cornelius! he said. The laundry! He rushed over and grabbed the bag as if to save any inconvenience. A grand day, Brother Cornelius said, taking it all in on the step. Just the ticket for the boys, Mr McKeown said nodding towards the path. Ah, off to the pictures, yes, a day out for good behaviour, Brother Cornelius chortled. Praise be to God, Mr McKeown said. He hurried towards the van, threw in the bag then raised his hand to take his leave.

The front door closed. Mr McKeown stood a moment inside to absorb the sound. He blessed himself. Then he walked up the dim hall without disclosure. He opened the kitchen door as if to surprise.   Glory be to God on high, he announced.   There was no sign of his wife. Nevertheless he concluded, And on earth peace to men of goodwill. He scanned all sides of the kitchen then closing the door he took off his laundry coat and hung it up on the hook. He smoothed back his hair and rubbed his hands together. Tut, tut.
A moment later Mrs McKeown came down the stairs just to be somewhere else. When she walked into the kitchen Mr McKeown gasped and put his hand on his chest. Mrs McKeown

walked past and into the scullery. She had not seen his face once that day. Ha-ha, Mr McKeown laughed left standing. He followed her to the scullery door. There you are, he said knowing she was somewhere in the early evening glimmer but exaggerating it. Mrs McKeown took risks. She began taking delft from a cupboard longer than was necessary, then meant every sound as she set it down. Mr McKeown spoke over it. Ah, now, sure the bad boys were taken to the pictures, he said. Mrs McKeown asked a question that she didn't intend, her head still lowered towards the delft. What bad boys? she drawled.

From the Home, Mr McKeown said as if it constituted a conversation then persisted, sure they were marched down to the Broadway two by two.

Mrs McKeown turned, immediately impressed, out of the gloom. Truly marvellous, she said, then cutely, Do you know how I could get a qualification to work with children?

Mr McKeown rocked on his heels. He moved back from the doorway to create more space. Work with children? he repeated loudly. Work with children? He paused then put his hand on his chin. Have those rapscallions been annoying you at that gable again? he asked bending forward in concern. I'll knock the socks off them, he added.

Mrs McKeown closed her eyes.

He was crucified for us, Mr McKeown said. And suffered under Pontius Pilate. He swung on his heels, noticing that the red lamp below the picture of the Sacred Heart had not yet been turned on. Or worse, had been turned off. And was buried, he emphasised, lunging at the switch. Mrs McKeown remained suspended, the sound of delft lost its purpose, the dim scullery no safety net.   I wish it was tea-time, she thought, otherwise what's the point of being together? She lifted a dish-cloth and rubbed a piece of grease from the stove to achieve perfection, then rinsed the cloth out of all proportion. She wrung it out and spread it on the draining-board. She adjusted a corner of it which was doubled in.   That's everything for the moment, she thought.

Mr McKeown got up from his knees blessing himself. He brushed the fronts of his trousers. The last supper, he said. Tut, tut. He paused on the spot before hurrying.   Then he had a revelation. He began opening the buttons of his shirt excitedly. He reached up and quietly lifted the edge of the picture of the Sacred Heart out from the wall. The bundle of notes fell into his hand. He looked down towards his vest then placed the money inside.   It fell about unsatisfactorily. Lord the night, he fumbled. He removed the notes and returned them to the picture. Buttoning up his shirt he went to the scullery door.

Mrs McKeown pretended she was doing something. She gave a sudden turn in a strange direction. Mr McKeown waited until she had finished then said, Could you sew a pocket in my inside-shirt?

Mrs McKeown made no apologies. She stared through the small scullery window like a view then turned it into a void by comparing it to every other view she had ever seen. For sheer closeness nothing touched it.

Woman, Mr McKeown projected adding, for the love of God,

Mrs McKeown swallowed shadow as the sun had no escape from brick. The straight yard wall told all, the faint-broken light narrowed to a horizon, the line between brick and brick. Suddenly Mrs McKeown set no limits. I'm taking a chair out into the yard, she announced, then planned her journey.

Mr McKeown stepped back, still slightly stooped in the scullery door. He tried to absorb the significance. Sweet body of Christ, he puzzled. He jiggled his knees in his trousers. He looked at his watch. Tut, tut. The chair gave some trouble as it passed by, it tipped a corner of the wall close to where Mr McKeown had graciously moved aside. He smarted, accused of existence, though he took no blame. He calculated his time of leaving for the monastery, then wound his watch. Mrs McKeown set the chair down at pains and opened the back door, taking all responsibility upon herself. Once in the yard she placed the chair where the sun still shone. She sat in the hard chair basked in upright isolation. I hope he's looking through the window, she thought. She raised her head to the lowering ray like death warmed-up, planning its next adventure.

Mr McKeown looked through the window. The back wall and the entry door no hindrance, nor his wife sun-bathing near the bin. Dominus vobiscum, he embraced. His voice hummed at that time of the day, the still light a moment's indecision. Then settled. He bowed his head. Et cum spiritu tuo.

Then there was a soft tap on the front door. Like the moment of truth Mr McKeown paused. Jesus, Mary and Joseph, he hesitated. He glanced this way and that. Finally his wife's oblivion in the sun proved too much. He rushed out through the back door. Mrs McKeown heard and took advantage. She raised her face a fraction further to the sky, her eyes lightly closed.

Immaculate Mary, Mr McKeown announced, there's somebody at the door.

Mrs McKeown pretended no reaction while vital time was lost. She heard the day slip to evening as her husband begged for mercy. Then she said quietly as if in a dream, Well, open it.

Mr McKeown swayed back speechless, the air in the yard mildly biding its time. Then he turned in one movement and cleared the scullery step while his wife hovered on the verge of capture.

Mr McKeown ejaculated under his breath as he approached the front door. Saint Matthew and all the saints. He shook his head several times. And martyrs. A few steps from the door the soft tap was repeated. Mr McKeown paused and let the hall commemorate its dullness. Then he stepped forward and swung the door open.

Ha-ha, he said throwing his head back confronted by a child. He stooped forward.

Saint Therese, he said. The Little Flower.

The child stood still and stared at him like any person at a door. Then spoke. As soon as she began Mr McKeown humoured her, his hands on his bent knees, a broad smile across his face. The child realised her full height and said her piece from beginning to end.

Would you like to sponsor me for a ten-mile walk?

Mr McKeown was incredulous of the apparition before him, of the fact that it had a voice. He stood up straight, put his hands on his hips and laughed in delight. The child stood on the spot and waited, a piece of paper and a pen in her hand. Behind, the street memorised the moment, houses rapt on the rim of spotlight.

Mr McKeown raised his hand suddenly by way of preservation. Don't move, he said. He turned on his heels and scuttled into the dim. The child stared into the open space and waited. Mr McKeown had no time to delay in the kitchen. It hung in the throes of abandon as he went straight through and out to the yard.

Mrs McKeown had barely savoured her escape.
Her husband broke the news, Hurry-up till you
see this.

What? she said. She cowered, the word hardly
audible.

At the door, in God's holy name, Mr McKeown
supplicated.

 Mrs McKeown burrowed into her chair. Then
she looked around the yard where the walls stood
stripped of excuse, the back door closed to the
entry. A hum of air held out for action. Mrs
McKeown considered the possibility of never
moving again. Mr McKeown adopted the pose of
anticipation. Divine light, he said.

He's left the scullery door open, Mrs McKeown
thought glancing sideways without protection.
She raised herself out of her chair. Mr McKeown
spun towards the door, taking the next step for
granted.

Mrs McKeown pattered through the kitchen. The
light hit on wallpaper, then it dazed on the floor.
Fate was more like it at the front door.   Mr
McKeown was already passing into the hall. Just
as he did he turned and twinkled his eyes at his
wife, she stopped and stared like a doleful dagger
then didn't want to make a scene. Mr McKeown
stood aside in the hallway to enhance the impact.
He looked towards the street and then at his wife.
The little Flower, he introduced. He bowed.

Framed by an edge of street-light the child stood.
Her face shone in shadow. Mrs McKeown's took
the full blare as she turned the corner, her anger

at her husband's trickery tight as skin. She stood where she was, a wealth of hall between her and the girl. How dare he, she thought, and me not qualified yet. Then she walked along the catwalk. When she reached the front door her husband peered over her shoulder and down at the child. The Little Flower, he said. Saint Therese. Tut, tut.

Mrs McKeown shuffled in her clothes then pretended equality. Well? she asked. Across the years she put on a brave smile. The child held out the piece of paper.

Would you sponsor me for a ten-mile walk?

Is the answer yes or no, Mrs McKeown thought. She stared across at crucial brick for inspiration, the sun worse than useless.

Bless my heart, Mr McKeown said, that's a long way. He swayed and almost touched his wife's back, as though they were one.

Which answer proves myself? Mrs McKeown considered.

You don't have to pay now, the child said. As shocking as that.

Ha-ha-ha, Mr McKeown laughed.

Mrs McKeown felt the thud of the ground she stood on, further than ever from the truth.

You just sign your name, the child continued, encouraged or losing confidence. She held out the pen.

Mr McKeown threw his head back like delirium. That's a good one, he raved, sign your name.

Mrs McKeown wanted a decision, she was embarrassed for both of them. She took the paper and pen, quickly signed her name in mid-air, and handed them back to the child. Crushed by her own bad signature she never wanted to be seen again.

But the child hadn't finished. She scrutinized the signature then offered the paper back. You didn't write how much, she said straight, her whole life ahead of her.

Too far down the road Mrs McKeown could only continue limply, asking directions along the way. How much? she repeated, her husband behind her in the outer reaches, repeating words and laughing continuously,   interposing prayers. Glory be to the Father, and soon after, and to the Son.

Then the child said, A mile.

How can you judge? Mrs McKeown wondered, her self-esteem still recoverable. Then she had an idea. I'll judge by the others, she thought. Let me see, she said and took the paper back. She recognised other names in the street. How much to make the child prefer me to them? she thought. But her husband had completed the calculations in his head. One penny, he said. It was the only sound in the street. Mrs McKeown salvaged the silence after. She filled in two pence.

The child took back the paper and pen and tripped across the street.

On the point of being heard or forgotten Mrs McKeown said, You'll be back then?- trailing off- for the money?

Holy virgin of virgins, Mr McKeown said. Ten miles. Sure she'll never finish that, what? You won't see her again.

Mrs McKeown stood on. Behind her, footsteps stuck to diminishment on oilcloth. In the strange space that followed, her body lost weight on the step or it was the time of the evening.

She stood on. It's a question of getting the information, she thought in the extension of a trance, and taking it from there.

House of gold

Cold hardened the air, then sounds softened it. Mrs McKeown stood at the back door looking out as if a dream had come true, its flagstones exuding whiteness. Snow is sent, she thought, to release you from the daily yard. She compared the scene to ordinary grey then stood stock still, not wanting to interrupt it or motionless under its spell. Whichever, she was already committed to its extreme. And it to hers.

Suddenly a sound came too close, a bang that had no right.

Unless I could move to the country, Mrs McKeown thought, annoyed, sure I've been in the city too long. She stepped out into the yard like a change of direction, her feet barely made a noise as each one sank deliberately towards the entry door. When she looked down the entry, merged into a pasture of snow, she abandoned her home. It would be obvious to anyone passing by, she thought, that I don't live here any more, I can stand as long as I want. She folded her arms.

See Amid the Winter Snow, Mr McKeown marvelled looking through the kitchen window. Tut, tut. Then he withdrew on the spot. What's that blessed woman doing? he wondered. He shook his head. The kitchen froze with removed solitude, the walls aghast at white. Mr McKeown shivered in his shoes, then stamped his feet. Jesus most admirable, he said. He hugged himself. Suddenly his wife was coming up the yard like a foreign traveller. The prodigal son, Mr McKeown remarked. He slit his eyes. He held his hands up by way of defence as a snowball spattered on the window-pane. He heard his wife laugh in blurred isolation. Queen of peace, he said, what's got into that woman? When she came in through the back door Mrs McKeown stamped the snow from her shoes on the scullery tiles not minding the consequences. She smoothed her skirt then looked around the walls of her old home. They dimmed in dereliction just familiar in the icy glimmer. Mr McKeown stood in the scullery doorway looking down at his wife in wonderment. Ha-ha, he said. You're enjoying the snow. He nodded his approval.

Mrs McKeown could not restrain herself. She raised her head slowly and, recognising her husband, said, How do you get a for-sale sign put up?

Mr McKeown staggered still. Then he bent double two ways. He shook his hands like a minstrel. A for-sale sign, he crooned, his face to the ceiling. A for-sale sign. Mrs McKeown stayed patiently in her place, awaiting the conclusion of the act. That's the best one yet, her husband applauded, then became serious. He bent towards her. Has that television next door been blaring again? he asked her. He twirled on his soles. I'll go in to them now, he said.

Mrs McKeown paused. The space behind her husband's back stopped short as he moved further away. Just as his hand touched the handle of the door she said in a voice almost too late, It's more than that.

Mr McKeown considered the closed door, then the pattern on the floor. As if it was impossible he turned slowly and said, In under God spell it out will you. What is it?

Everything, Mrs McKeown whispered starting up a new relationship out of the blue, the universe the limit. She stood on her own.

Mr McKeown lacked the time. His body confronted itself in several directions. Tut, tut, he said. He loosened his collar then consulted his watch. Kyrie eleison, he said picturing the altar. Then he asked his wife, Will I go in to them or what?

But Mrs McKeown had remembered to wash her hands. She was at the sink where running water drowned out the difference. When she looked through the window and saw the snow swept against the brick wall she thought, A little bungalow underneath the mountains would be nice. Looking out on the sea. When she pulled the hand- towel from the back door she was released from its memory. It has no place in my new life, she thought regarding it with a cold eye. Then she raised it to her nose and smelt it. I can't believe I've put up with that smell for so long, she thought comparing it to the open air. Then she opened the back door and walked out into radiant white. She hung the towel on the line though it could not make the journey. She stood still, frozen in the act of belonging to a scene, while separately, muffled sounds constructed it.

Mr McKeown muttered throughout. Mirror of justice, he beseeched, give me strength. He flitted on one side of the window, his wife a mirage on the other. He shook his head. Tut, tut. Then he seized the moment. He disappeared. The next moment he was at the small tin on the sideboard prising it open. He drew breath as if terrified, the sound of tin enough. Then his eyes glinted. Ha-ha, he said. He withdrew a number of coins and slipped them into his pocket. He replaced the lid like a glove then delighted, went to straighten himself. Mrs McKeown said nothing standing looking in from the open door, the air laden with it. Mr McKeown half-turned, caught her in the side of his eye then feigning embarrassment, laughed out of place. You're the one, he said tapping his pocket. The limit. Tut, tut.

Mrs McKeown turned and closed the door then faced the scullery air. Everywhere has nowhere to go, she thought looking at still objects, in comparison to moving house, sure I've been here too long. How did I put up with it? She lifted the kettle from the stove in the meantime. And filled it. I'll have a cup of tea, she thought, to warm me up, and plan the future. Soon the kettle purred like comfort. In the distance she heard her husband stabbing the fire, the wound glowed long after. She went to the doorway. She watched him bask in the flames' admiration. From this angle, she thought and it irritated her, I can't help feeling sorry for his back.

Mr McKeown replaced the poker. He clapped his hands. Ye holy angels, he said. He took a step back and put his hands to his cheeks. And archangels, he added. He could not believe the fire before him. Miraculous, he exclaimed turning and seeing his wife in the doorway. He didn't know which way to look so he wallowed from one to the other. His wife brought him down gently.

Would you mind brushing the hearth, she said. She smiled slightly with mystery while her husband dived at the companion set. Mother of God, he remarked. You don't want much. Then he brushed the ashes into a neat little heap at the side of the grate. As he hung the silver brush back on its stand Mrs McKeown said, What good's that?

Mr McKeown looked at the heap of ashes, then at his wife. He took a step back and adjusted his collar. Mrs McKeown watched him scorch briefly then explained, The ashes go underneath the grate, not beside it.

Christ the night, Mr McKeown said, I'll be late for the Confraternity. Then he bent down and lifted the little brush from the stand. Holding his face away from the heat he manoeuvred the ashes into the side of the grate where he dispersed them quickly so that they might not be noticed.

There, he said, replacing the brush. Ha-ha.

Mrs McKeown seemed rooted to the spot, then engulfed by it. Before her Mr McKeown swayed back and forth as if performing a ritualistic dance. She forgot what he was doing there. Once you've made a decision, she thought, how do you live every day? Mr McKeown turned suddenly. He began to rush. In God's holy name, he exclaimed battling his way through the steam, where are you woman? I'm here, Mrs McKeown said distantly. Mr McKeown hurried past her and swung the back door open. He shooed the steam out, then rescued the kettle from the stove. He wiped his brow like a hero. Phew! he said. Tut, tut.

Mrs McKeown made her way over to the fireplace. She removed the front of the grate and brushed the ashes in. She replaced the front of the grate and the brush, then stood back to remark the difference. Taking her time she crossed the floor to the scullery where by chance she met her husband at the sink. New-fangled they didn't know what to say. Mr McKeown shook his head. Then Mrs McKeown timed it perfectly. As soon as he removed the kettle from the running water she darted her hands underneath causing no complications. Mr McKeown walked round the back of her and placed the kettle on the stove. He reached out for the open door. Merciful God, he said pulling it closed.   He shivered.   He went back to the kitchen, livening things up as he went.   That's a cold one, he said. Brrr.

Mrs McKeown turned on the gas again without consultation.   The tension in the scullery a lifetime's work, it seemed to peel away.   The kettle started up like a distant train.   Mrs McKeown stepped onto the platform though the train was not in sight.   The thing about me is, she thought, I never stay in the one place long.   She looked across at her husband from the scullery door.   He was bent down by the fire warming his hands, still in the vicinity.

Would you be joining me in the buffet?   Mrs McKeown asked leaning against the train door as it pulled out of the station.

What? Mr McKeown jumped back on the kitchen floor.

I said is this your station?

What?   Mr McKeown balanced himself.   He checked the coins in his pocket. Satisfied that he knew them by touch he consulted his watch.   Of the cross? he asked ruffling around then added, between that blessed hearth and you and your games-.

As he rushed across to the kitchen door Mrs McKeown still hadn't decided whether or not to take him with her.   It's touch and go, she thought.   When the front door stung closed and silence winced after she thought, go.   Then on the brink of defection she turned and going into the scullery switched the gas off.

Mr McKeown paused outside the front door. He beat his chest three times. Almighty God, he said. He looked around the street where twilight barely touched the snow, animating it. He bowed his head. Be merciful onto us, he added. Children's voices chinked, altar lights to Mr McKeown's ears. He felt the blaze in his chest, his eyes simple with pleasure. Everything confirmed what he knew, the scheme of things no shock. He fixed his scarf, then pulled up his collar. He put his hands in his pockets and adopted a lurching stance then picked his steps through the felt snow. Divine grace, he said. He chuckled. When he came to the other side of the street he bent down to look for the pavement. Where in God's name does one thing end and the other begin? he wondered. Ha-ha. He pressed around gently with his foot until he touched the edge. Alleluia, he said ascending the few inches onto the pavement. Tut, tut. The monastery bell rang out, the entry ahead a moment between. When Mr McKeown walked into it his feet crunched like stars landing. Tower of ivory, he ejaculated looking downward lest he lose his balance. When he came to the exit he paused to glance around the street before heading on. Windows peeped over snow-packed windowsills. Children clumped lightly on the road, their dark figures dazzled. Mr McKeown adjusted his hat. House of gold, he said. He bent forward and waded across the street diagonally left.

Mrs McKeown went up the stairs to make a start. If I don't do something practical, she thought, I'll get nowhere. She went into her bedroom and turned on the light, the bare bulb no preparation. She looked around the walls, the wallpaper drab with rejection, then at the top of the wardrobe where a large suitcase sat bereft of holiday.

How can I reach that case, she wondered. On the point of giving up she went over to the side of the bed and lifted a chair. With tribal dignity she carried it over to the wardrobe, set it down and climbed up onto it. Her fingers just touched the suitcase pushing it further back towards the wall, where it shrugged its lid then settled.

How did that happen? Mrs McKeown stared at it in the way of an exalted piece of tripped-over pavement.

She looked around the room. Her eyes fell with disdain on meagre possessions, turning them into life. What does it amount to? she thought. She felt weak with the past. Just on the point of dismounting she caught sight of a walking-stick in the corner. She thought momentarily of Mr McKeown's sore back, but she had a better idea. She got down from the chair and hurried over and lifted the stick. Going back over to the wardrobe she pushed the suitcase with the stick until it fell on the floor. She was prepared for a noise but not the noise it made.

Mrs McKeown stared into the meaning of an empty suitcase then wondered what to pack first.

She looked from one part of the room to another but nothing obvious struck her. Either I would have to take it out again to use it, she thought looking for example at a hairbrush, or it mightn't be worth taking at all. Her eyes lit on an old tea-tin sitting on the windowsill. I'll start with that, she thought. She hurried over and took off the lid. It was filled with a variety of bits and pieces. Mrs McKeown shook the tin several times but each time it settled it was all the same, nothing decisive was at the top. Finally she carried the tin over to the bed and emptied all the contents onto the quilt. She spread them out.

Do something, she implored them. She spread them out further, separating buttons from paper-clips, old keys from curtain hooks. Mrs McKeown regarded them critically then sat down on the bed where finally the stuff of a home became the remains of the future. Decisively and swiftly she gathered the bits and pieces into a pile and replaced them in the tin. She carried the tin over and put it back on the windowsill. Returning to the bed, she brushed debris carefully off the quilt, trying to catch it in her other hand. Then she looked at her cold hand. Where are you supposed to put this dust? she wondered glancing around the room as if doubt had escaped from the tin. She crossed over to the light-switch and turned off the light. Then plans if they existed were a part of general dark, the suitcase an obstacle on the way. She picked her steps to the window. With one hand she flicked aside the curtain and with the same hand pushed the window up. She held both hands out and lightly brushed the debris into the night air where plucky particles glistened briefly as they vanished. Snow trapped the street like a story-book, the cover lingering on. Mrs McKeown looked at the rooftops where moonlight skimmed white with a hint of black beyond the edge. At that point it mentioned life.

Mr McKeown was loath to leave the warmth of the monastery. He sat in his seat while throngs shuffled down the aisles. He prayed for his fellow man while he waited for the monastery to clear. Blasts of cold air came from the open doors. Mr McKeown shuddered in his coat. He raised his eyes to the ornate roof. Deliver us, we beseech Thee, he prayed. He turned and gave a deadly glance at the commotion going through the swing doors, then faced the altar again. From all evils past present and to come, he added. Then the doors swung shut for the last time. Mr McKeown allowed the silence to celebrate in silence. He bowed his head. Suddenly he felt dissatisfied with his position. I'm too far back, he thought. He sidled out and hurried up towards the altar. He genuflected. He went into the front pew and placed his hat on the seat beside him. He knelt down and joined his hands on the rail in front. Ahead of him the tabernacle glowed like an invitation home. Mr McKeown accepted without hesitation. He offered up thanksgiving.

Then in the side of his eye he saw a priest coming out of the vestry, a priest coming across the altar and down the steps, his head held harmlessly to the side, his feet soundless as souls. Mr McKeown, spurred on, accelerated his whispering. He rolled his eyes. The priest passed him by, a bunch of keys jingling softly in his hand. Then he stopped thoughtfully and, turning back approached Mr McKeown.

Mr McKeown, he said quietly, would you be willing to take on an extra duty?

Oh, surely surely Father, Mr McKeown answered too quickly for the words he said.

In the vestry, the priest said.

Mr McKeown could not believe his ears. That he should be allowed into the inner sanctum of the church was beyond his wildest prayers. He bowed his head humbly, then raised it respectfully.

Come to the vestry after devotions tomorrow evening, the priest said. He touched Mr McKeown's joined hand.

Mrs McKeown looked down the entry along the flattened snow. None had fallen overnight. Morning light bared the cold, high walls guarded it. In between, the pathway lay deserted down to the end where another wall stood opposite. Mrs McKeown left her empty home and stepped out into the entry. She paused and tightened her woollen hat around her ears. Then sounds came cushioned over rooftops, they landed like snowballs in the air. Mrs McKeown walked on the white surface, her fur-lined boots gripped the snow that lay close to the wall. Then she heard a clang from a neighbouring yard and renewed her effort. Just when it seemed worthwhile a voice felled her close to her own back door. I have to keep my mind on the goal, she thought, otherwise I'm exposed to every blow. When she reached the bottom of the entry she turned right.

Suddenly houses opened up before her causing just enough space for the journey ahead. A gleam of light caught the possibility of things. Compared with where they were. She stopped still at the street corner. Imagine, she thought, where I'm going, then headed down the hill in the direction of the main road. I'm sure, she thought, there's an estate agent's there, then pictured it. Meantime life went on around her, busy at that time of the day. Mrs McKeown fluttered in her coat, she rose in her boots. The main road drummed its glove-beat, accompanying plans that marched away.

Then she was on it and turned left. I can't see from here, she thought, but I imagine it along that row of shops. She passed people going about with the poise of the everyday. Decisions are enough, she thought, to walk amongst them. She floated on the pavement where the snow was turning to slush. Soon she reached a small window in between a newsagents and a fruit shop, in which were displayed photographs of houses. She stopped abruptly, shocked at the suddenness of her arrival. Goodness, she thought, is this it? Immediately exposed she put on an act, the front of the road no background. She glanced around at the hollowness of it then tried to concentrate on the houses in front of her. Soon they were familiar, drab replicas of where she lived. She examined addresses. But, she realised, these are all houses round about. There are no mountains. No sea. She moved along to the door of the shop and peered in, a man sat behind a desk, in front of him a young couple. Mrs McKeown had a sudden attack of where she was then hid in front of the glass. Rigid with it all she turned her back on the shop and looked up and down the road. Committing herself to an instant lifestyle she stepped out purposefully in the direction from which she had come. That was close, she thought in general or particular.

A little way on she remembered she had to get some food. There's no way round it, she thought as though a further trap had just been sprung. She turned in at the door of a small self-service store. A bright bulb glared and shelves stood in straight rows ahead. Mrs McKeown lifted a basket and started to walk up an aisle. Cold-hearted she removed items from shelves and proceeded to the till. Around her, people spoke in their ordinary voices. In her head she practised hers then, when she got to the till, affected it. Perfectly timed she said, Thank you, with a smile.

Once outside, she glanced around then set off for the corner. Cold twinkled on ice, the blade-filled air scraped lightly.   Traffic skimmed heavily along, it dodged her about the dazzled surface of the   pavement.   Mrs   McKeown   drew   an exhilarated   breath   in.   Then   let   it   out.   She glowed.